A Chinese Ishmael
and Other Stories

Sui Sin Far

CONTENTS

A CHINESE ISHMAEL

IN THE light of night, on the detached rocks near the Cliff House, the sea-lions are clambering and growling; the waters of the Pacific are foaming around them, and their young, in the clefts of the rookeries, are drifting into dreamland on lullabies sung by the waves.

Mark that great fellow ensconced on a rocky pedestal. Why does he roar so restlessly and complainingly? I wonder, if he could speak, if he would tell where Leih Tseih and Ku Yum lie. I almost fancy that he sees the lovers quiet and still under the waters.

Ku Yum leant over the balcony of the big lodging-house on Dupont Street. She was very tired, for she was a delicate little thing and her tiny hands and feet were kept moving all day; her mistress had a heart like a razor and a tongue to match. Underneath the balcony there passed a young man, and as he went by, some spirit whispered in Ku Yum's ear, "Let fall a Chinese lily."

Ku Yum obeyed the spirit, and the young man, whose name was Leih Tseih, raised his eyes, and seeing Ku Yum, loved her. The Chinese lily he lifted from the ground and carried it away in his sleeve. Thereafter every day, going backward and forward to his work, Leih Tseih passed under the balcony where he had first seen Ku Yum, but the maiden no longer leaned over the railing. She had grown shy, and contented herself with peeping out of the door of the upper room. At last Leih Tseih, who was beside himself with love, threw her a note wrapped around a stone. Ku Yum caught and demurely retired with it; but just as she was placing it in the sole of her shoe her mistress came behind her and twisted it out of her fingers.

"You wicked, wicked thing!" cried the woman. "How dare you keep company with a bad man!"

Poor little Ku Yum's transparent face flushed.

"If I am a wicked thing, a bad man is fit company for me," she cried. "But he who wrote me that is a superior man."

At that her mistress fell to beating her with a little switch. Ku Yum screamed; but instead of receiving help, her mistress's husband appeared and relieved his wife as switcher, having a stronger arm.

There lived on the floor just below the Lee Chus, the owners of Ku Yum, a woman who had compassion on the slave-girl. She too had seen Leih Tseih pass and the tossing up of the note, and had said to herself, "Now, there are a fine-looking young man and a pearl of a girl becoming acquainted. May they be happy!"

So when Ku Yum's screams rent the air, her heart swelled big with pity, and though she dared not interfere between mistress and maid, she resolved to watch for Leih Tseih and tell him what she knew concerning Ku Yum.

When Leih Tseih learned what had befallen the girl of his heart for his sake, the blood rushed to his head, and he would have leapt up the stairs and carried Ku Yum away by force, but A-Chuen, the woman, restrained him, saying: "Be discreet, and I will assist you; be rash, and you will lose all."

"But," demurred Leih Tseih, "if a man will not enter a tiger's lair, how can he obtain her whelps?"

"By coaxing them out," replied A-Chuen.

Then the woman and the young man conferred together, and it came to pass that when the stars were in the sky, Ku Yum, in a peach-colored blouse, a present from a cousin in China, stood with downcast eyes in A-Chuen's sitting-room and listened to words from her lover. She could not be induced to look at Leih Tseih, but he caught the shine of her eyes underneath the lids, and thought her as sweet as a li-chee.

"Dear child," said A-Chuen, "do not tremble so; you are with friends."

Then Leih Tseih told how he had planned to remove her from the people who had treated her so cruelly. A-Chuen, who had an old husband who loved her well enough to do all that she wished, would leave the house on Dupont Street and take a small house for herself. There Ku Yum should safely abide. Meanwhile, A-Chuen with amiable and flattering words would induce the Lee Chus to allow Ku Yum to come to A-Chuen's room to work some embroidery on garments for her husband's store, thereby preventing Ku Yum from being abused.

"You are very good and very kind," responded Ku Yum. "But unless I am bought from the Lee Chus, I cannot leave them. I have heard them talking of an offer that Lum Choy has made for me. It is dollars and dollars, and before many moons go by I fear I shall be obliged to be his."

"Who is Lum Choy?" asked Leih Tseih, his face white with anger and surprise.

"He is a very ugly man," said Ku Yum, "and there is a scar right across his forehead. But he has made money, they say, in more ways than the way of labor."

"And you wish to be sold to him?" queried Leih Tseih jealously.

"That I did not say," replied Ku Yum, "but this I do say: I am only a slave, but still a Chinese maiden. He is a man who, wishing to curry favor with the white people, wears American clothes, and when it suits his convenience passes for a Japanese."

"Shame on him!" cried A-Chuen.

"Kind friend," said Leih Tseih to A-Chuen, "if you so please, I would speak to Ku Yum alone."

3

A-Chuen left the room, and Leih Tseih, seating himself beside Ku Yum said, "I would like to tell you of myself."

"What you like to tell, I like to hear," replied Ku Yum.

"Then, listen," said Leih Tseih. "I am the son of a high mandarin, but being possessed of a turbulent and unruly spirit I ran away from home in my eighteenth year and through the agency of the Six Companies came to San Francisco. Here I obtained work, but the Gambling Cash Tiger had all of my thoughts, and it came to pass in the heat of a game, when I saw my adversary, the very Lum Choy you speak of, playing me false, that I struck at him with a knife and left him lying wounded. I escaped punishment and followed a seafaring-man's life for several years. Then came shipwreck and drifting for days alone upon the mighty waters, and my soul at last was humbled; and one solemn night, when naught could be heard save the washing of the waves against the side of my small boat, I acknowledged with sorrow to the Parent of All that I had indeed wandered far from the path of virtue, and vowed, if my life were spared, to follow my conscience, — for I had indeed been the bad man your mistress called me."

"Good or bad," cried little Ku Yum, "you are you and I am I." And she patted his hand shyly to show that what she had heard had not changed her feelings. Then she added, "And now I vow I will never be Lum Choy's, but ever yours, who have the grace of the well-born."

Leih Tseih smiled and exclaimed, "What a woman!" and declared that he loved every inch of her skin and the spirit that dwelt behind her eyes.

"I was picked up by a sailing-vessel bound for San Francisco," continued Leih Tseih, "and since returning to this city, I have conformed to virtue in every respect. I sought work and I obtained it. I have saved money — almost sufficient to pay to the Six Companies the amount of my indebtedness. It was with the object of relieving myself of that obligation that I saved. But now, my Ku Yum, that sum will take you and me together far away from here to another city on the other side of this world. What do you say?"

Little Ku Yum shook her head.

"I told my mistress," said she, "that you were a superior man."

"So be it," returned Leih Tseih, rebuked, "I will take the punishment I deserve, and after my debt has been paid will wait for you until I have made money enough to buy you."

"No; when you have paid your debt and are able to take me away, I will fly with you wherever and whenever you wish."

"Even though I steal you."

"That I will consider a righteous theft. Besides, the sooner you are out of this city the better. Are you not afraid that you may be recognized and thrown into prison?"

Note: illustration omitted

"I am not afraid. Life on the ocean transformed me both inwardly and outwardly."

"That may be, but I fear for you now. Be careful, I pray you. If you meet Lum Choy there will be trouble; and should he become aware that you and I have met, he would be a bloodhound on your track."

"Well, for your sake I will watch and be cautious."

When A-Chuen reappeared, Leih Tseih said, "Kind woman, we have agreed when the proper time comes to seek another city where we can be united. Here there are laws to separate us, but none to bind."

Which was true; for how could Leih Tseih and Ku Yum ask either Chinese priest or American in San Francisco to make them man and wife?

"One might as well look for a pin at the bottom of the ocean," growled Lum Choy.

He spoke to the Lee Chus, who had been vainly searching for weeks for Ku Yum.

"Well, it may be that she has given herself to the sea," answered Lee Chu, who was not very bright.

"Imbeciles!" was his wife's quick rejoinder as she snapped her eyes at the men. "A girl with a new lover can always be found — by him."

"What do you mean?" asked Lum Choy.

"Why, this: Ku Yum had a lover who passed here every day. It is to his embraces, not to those of cold water that Ku Yum has given herself. The shameful thing! If I had her here I would tear her eyes out."

Lum Choy's face had become livid.

"Do you know this man?" said he. "If so, I will trace her through him."

"I should know him were I to see him," said Lee Chu's wife, "but he has not passed for three or four weeks. I had the letter which he wrote to Ku Yum, but the girl stole it from me before she left."

"He will pass again," replied Lum Choy. "Ku Yum is not here now, so he does not make this his way. But he must pass some time. Tell me the hour when he was wont to go by and I will watch day after day and never weary until I have run him down."

The presidents of the Six Companies had met together in the council hall.

The chief of the Sam Yups, an imposing man with thought-refined features, was urging the advisability of expending a sum of money for the relief of some sick laborers, when a rapping was heard, followed by the entrance of the Six Companies' secretary, who approached the aged chief of the Hop Wos and whispered a few words in his ear.

"You can admit him," responded the old man.

The secretary left the room, and in a few minutes returned with a repulsive-looking fellow whose forehead bore a huge scar.

"This is Lum Choy," announced the secretary.

"Well," Lum Choy, what is your complaint?" inquired the Hop Wo chief.

"My complaint," said Lum Choy, in a high, rasping voice, "is that living in this city is a man named Leih Tseih, who owes this honorable body the cost of his transportation from China to America, and as well sundry other taxes. His debt is of many years' standing, yet he works as a free man and himself receives the good of every cent he earns. More than this, Leih Tseih is a fugitive criminal, having some five years ago assaulted a man with murderous intent and escaped the consequences of his crime. I, Lum Choy, am the man he assaulted, and bear on my forehead the mark of his knife. I also complain that this Leih Tseih has abducted a slave girl named Ku Yum, or rather, stolen her from one Lee Chu, and that he has secreted her in a house on Stockton Street, to which I can lead you. And I petition that you engage officers of the law to capture this lawless man, and that you prosecute him, as it is in order for the Six Companies so to do."

There were a few seconds of silence after Lum Choy had finished speaking; then the Sam Yup chief arose. He regarded gravely the mean figure of Lum Choy, and said: "Presidents of the Yeong Wo, Kong Chow, Yan Wo, Hop Wo and Ning Yeong Societies, you may remember that less than one month ago I delivered over to the Six

Companies' Fund a sum of money, which, as I then stated, had been paid to me by one of our delinquent emigrants, whose name I had been requested by him to withhold. You did not press me to reveal that name, but the time has come to do so. The man who paid me that money was Leih Tseih, and the amount, as shown [illustration omitted] in our books, covers the whole of his indebtedness. We, therefore, have no legal claim against Leih Tseih, and are not authorized to punish him for the deeds which Lum Choy has charged him with."

Lum Choy could not restrain himself. "What!" he cried, "the powerful Six Companies have no jurisdiction over the men they have brought to this country?"

"In some cases we have," replied the Hop Wo chief suavely; "but this case lies with the American courts. Although so many years have elapsed since Leih Tseih assaulted you, I believe you still have recourse against him, and as you are one of our men, we will certainly do what we can to assist you in avenging yourself according to law."

"But the slave girl, Ku Yum?"

"Are you interested in her?" queried the Sam Yup.

"I am," returned Lum Choy. "I have paid a large sum for her, which Lee Chu will not refund, and it was on the day that she was to have come to me that she fled with Leih Tseih. In my search for her I discovered the man, and I have made no mistake, for day after day, night after night, I have dogged his footsteps."

The chief of the Ning Yeongs then said: "Lum Choy has suffered grievous wrongs, and we must do all in our power to assist him in bringing his wronger to justice; but the purchase of slave-girls, which is just and right in our own country, is not lawful in America. Therefore, the task of recovering Ku Yum cannot be undertaken by the Six Companies. It must be intrusted to the hands of private parties and conducted secretly. Otherwise Lum Choy and Lee Chu will have as much to answer for, according to the law of this country, as had Leih Tseih."

"And," rejoined the Sam Yup president, "that being so, I would advise Lum Choy to let matters rest. He who strives for a woman makes much trouble for himself. Besides, is it not better to forgive an injury than to avenge one?"

"Great and noble are your sentiments, benevolent Sam Yup chief," broke in Lum Choy, with a scarcely concealed sneer; "but they are not the sentiments of a man who has been injured as I have been, and I will have vengeance if it costs me my life."

With these words he left the council-room. Desire for a woman, hate for a man, had changed the nature of the once shrewd and clear-headed Lum Choy, and his mind was fired with one idea — vengeance.

"If," meditated he in the darkness of midnight, "I imprison Leih Tseih for a few months, perhaps a year, Ku Yum will be his at the end of that time and love him more than ever. If I use secret means to obtain Ku Yum, and do obtain her, the sweetness of the fruit will not be for me, for her mind and heart will be with my rival. If I kill Leih Tseih, Ku Yum's spirit will follow his, for that is the way with women who dare what she has dared. What, then, can I do to satisfy myself and draw Ku Yum's heart from Leih Tseih? This only — kill Lum Choy and make Leih Tseih his murderer. Oho! devils, I shall soon be one of you! And now I must arrange so that he shall be the last person with me. I know where I can obtain a knife of his, and I know how I can lure him here. He will be overjoyed with my offer to relinquish my claim on Ku Yum for a small tax on his weekly wages, and while he is pouring out his gratitude to me for abandoning my vengeance, I will dabble him well with blood from a cut arm. He must come here in the dusk of the evening and immediately after his departure, the deed will be done. Ha, ha! what a revenge!"

"Your eyes are strange; there is blood on your garments!" cried Ku Yum to Leih Tseih, who without warning had appeared before her.

Leih Tseih's set face relaxed.

"Be not afraid, my bird," said he; "but to-night you and I must part."

"Part! O, no, no!" She sprang to his side and caught his hand.

"It is true. I am hunted again. Lum Choy has been found dead with a knife in his heart. I was the last person seen to enter his room. And as you see, my garments are blood-stained."

For a second the girl shrank back; then, alas for the lost soul of Lum Choy, pressed closer to her lover and whispered in his ear, "If all men save Leih Tseih were killed by Leih Tseih, still would Ku Yum remain with Leih Tseih."

"I am unworthy," murmured Leih Tseih, brokenly. "Though I am guiltless of the deed for which I know they will condemn me, yet my past has been such that it justifies the condemnation. But you, O sweetest heart! you must forget me!"

Ku Yum shook her head. "I can die, but I cannot do what you have asked of me."

Some silent seconds, then Leih Tseih said in a clear voice, "We will die together — you and I."

"Ah! that will be happiness — to enter the spirit-land, hand in hand. When my cousins in China hear of it, they will say, 'How fine! Our cousin, Ku Yum, who was a slave-girl on earth, walks the Halls of Death with the son of a high mandarin.'"

To the Cliff they sped. Arrived where from a parapet they could leap into the Pacific, they embraced tenderly and were gone. None can point to the spot where life with all its troubles ended, for their bodies were never found; but in that part of San Francisco called the City of the Chinese it is whispered from lip to ear that the spirits of Leih Tseih and Ku Yum have passed into a pair of beautiful sea-lions who wander in the moonlight over the rocks, meditating on life and love and sorrow.

AN AUTUMN FAN

FOR two weeks Ming Hoan was a guest in the house of Yen Chow, the father of Ah Leen, and because love grows very easily between a youth and a maid it came to pass that Ah Leen unconsciously yielded to Ming Hoan her heart and Ming Hoan as unconsciously yielded his to her. After the yielding they became conscious.

When their tale was told to Yen Chow he was much disturbed, and vowed that he would not disgrace his house by giving his daughter to a youth whose parents had betrothed him to another.

"How canst thou help it if thy daughter loves me and becomes my wife?" boldly answered Ming Hoan. "We are in America, and the fault, if fault there be, is not upon thy shoulders."

"True!" murmured the mother of Ah Leen, smiling upon her would-be-son-in-law. "America!" Yen Chow shook his head. "Land where a man knows no law save his own — where even a son of China forgets his ancestors and follows his human heart."

"Sir!" returned Ming Hoan, "when the human heart is linked to the divine, ought we not to follow thereafter?"

There was much more said, but it all ended in the young people wedding — and parting. For that was Chow's stern decree. Ming Hoan must face his parents and clear away the clouds of misunderstanding before he could take Ah Leen.

And now Ming Hoan is gone and Ah Leen stands alone. Her mother enters the room. Ah Leen must have some tea. The wife of Yen Chow leads her daughter into the wide hall, where refreshments are laid. The usual ceremonies attendant upon a wedding, and which in the case of Ah Leen's cousins, Ah Toy and Mai Gwi Far, had lasted over a week, were to be postponed until Ming Hoan's return from China.

Her mother congratulates her. Ming Hoan is good to behold, wise beyond his years and had seen the face of the world. His fortune is not large, but it will grow. Most comforting thought of all, there will be no mother-in-law to serve or obey. Ming Hoan's home for many years to come will be in the great City of New York.

See, there is Ah Chuen, the wife of the herb doctor, and Sien Tau, the mother of the president of the Water Lily Society. They are coming to wish her felicity. Mark the red paper they are scattering on the way. They are good-natured women, and even if their class is below that of the wife of Yen Chow, their gifts prove natural refinement. Thus Ah Leen's mother.

"Mother," murmurs Ah Leen, "I beg that you will kindly excuse me to our friends."

She carries her tea to the veranda, and, seated in a bamboo rocker, muses on Ming Hoan. She is both happy and sad. Happy to be a bride, yet sad because alone.

It had been a strange ceremony — that wedding. It is not customary, even in America, for a Chinese bride to remain under her father's roof, and only because, in his bended arm, she had wept her tears away, could Ah Leen realize herself the wife of Ming Hoan.

How beautiful the day! Above her a deep blue dome, paling as it descends to the sea. Around her curving, sloping hills, covered with a tender green; here and there patches of glowing, dazzling color — California flowers. It is spring-time — the springtime of the year. A little carol of joy escapes Ah Leen's lips. It is good to love and be loved even if —

What is that Lee A-Chuen is saying? "'Tis a pity that Yen Chow should have sent the bridegroom away. Youth is youth and soon forgets. The sister of my mother writes me that the choice of his parents is the loveliest of all the lovely girls in the Provinces of the Rippling Rivers." The day has suddenly darkened for Ah Leen.

Five moons have gone by since Ming Hoan went over the sea, and no letter — no message — not even a word has come to his waiting bride. But it is whispered in all the Chinese merchants' families that Ming Hoan, disregarding his first marriage, which, being unconsented to by his parents, could scarcely be considered binding, had taken to himself as wife in his own land Fi Shui, the daughter of his father's friend.

The cousins of Ah Leen regard her with pitying looks whilst they whisper among themselves, "An autumn fan! An autumn fan!"

Ah Leen meets them with a serene countenance. Her American friend suggests that she should obtain a divorce; that that is the only course open for a deserted wife who wishes to retain her self-respect.

"A deserted wife!" echoes Ah Leen. "Ah, no; 'twas my father who compelled him to leave me. And what has he done that I should divorce him? Men cannot live upon memories, and it is perfectly right and proper, since he has decided to remain in China, that he should take to himself another wife."

At the time of the year when the heavens weep, as the Chinese say, there comes news of the birth of a son to Ming Hoan.

Again the American girl watches sympathetically the face of the first wife of the man to whom a son has been born by another woman. Sun Lin, wife of the Sam Yup Chief, brings the news to the house of Yen Chow. It is sundown and the American girl is sitting on the porch with Ah Leen.

"Joy!" cries Ah Leen. "My husband has a son!"

And she herself, on red note paper, sends news of the event to those of her friends who have not yet heard of it. These notes are proudly signed: "Ming Ah Leen, First Wife of Ming Hoan."

The year rolls on. There comes to the house of Yen Chow a Chinese merchant of wealth and influence. His eyes dwell often upon Ah

Leen. He whispers to her father. Yen Chow puffs his pipe and muses: Assuredly a great slight has been put upon his family. A divorce would show proper pride. It was not the Chinese way, but was not the old order passing away and the new order taking its place? Aye, even in China, the old country that had seemed as if it would ever remain old. He speaks to Ah Leen.

"Nay, father, nay," she returns. "Thou hadst the power to send my love away from me, but thou canst not compel me to hold out my arms to another."

"But," protests her mother, "thy lover hath forgotten thee. Another hath borne him a child."

A flame rushes over Ah Leen's face; then she becomes white as a water lily. She plucks a leaf of scented geranium, crushes it between her fingers and casts it away. The perfume clings to the hands she lays on her mother's bosom.

"Thus," says she, "the fragrance of my crushed love will ever cling to Ming Hoan."

It is evening. The electric lights are shining through the vines. Out of the gloom beyond their radius comes a man. The American girl, seated in a quiet corner of the veranda, sees his face. It is eager and the eyes are full of love and fate. Then she sees Ah Leen. Tired of woman's gossip, the girl has come to gaze upon the moon, hanging in the sky above her like a pale yellow pearl.

There is a cry from the approaching man. It is echoed by the girl. In a moment she is leaning upon his breast.

"Ah!" she cries, raising her head and looking into his eyes. "I knew that though another had bound you by human ties, to me you were linked by my love divine."

"Another! Human ties!" exclaims the young man. He exclaims without explaining — for the sins of parents must not be uncovered

— why there has been silence between them for so long. Then he lifts her face to his and gently reproaches her. "Ah Leen, you have dwelt only upon your love for me. Did I not bid thee, 'Forget not to remember that *I* love thee!'"

The American girl steals away. The happy Ming Hoan is unaware that as she flits lightly by him and his bride she is repeating to herself his words, and hoping that it is not too late to send to someone a message of recall.

THE BIRD OF LOVE

I

THEY were two young people with heads hot enough and hearts true enough to believe that the world was well lost for love, and they were Chinese.

They sat beneath the shade of a cluster of tall young pines forming a perfect bower of greenness and coolness on the slope of Strawberry hill. Their eyes were looking oceanwards, following a ship nearing the misty horizon. Very loving yet very serious were their faces and voices. That ship, sailing from west to east, carried from each a message to his and her kin — a message which humbly but firmly set forth that they were resolved to act upon their belief and to establish a home in the new country, where they would ever pray for blessings upon the heads of those who could not see as they could see nor hear as they could hear.

"My mother will weep when she reads," sighed the girl.

"Pau Tsu," the young man asked, "Do you repent?"

"No," she replied, "But — "

She drew from her sleeve a letter written on silk paper.

The young man ran his eye over the closely penciled characters.

"'Tis very much in its tenor like what my father wrote to me," he commented.

"Not that."

Pau Tsu indicated with the tip of her pink forefinger a paragraph which read:

17

"Are you not ashamed to confess that you love a youth who is not yet your husband? Such disgraceful boldness will surely bring upon your head the punishment you deserve. Before twelve moons go by, you will be an Autumn Fan."

The young man folded the missive and returned it to the girl whose face was averted from his.

"Our parents," said he, "knew not love in its springing and growing, its bud and blossom. Let us, therefore, respectfully read their angry letters, but heed them not. Shall I not love you dearer and more faithfully because you became mine at my own request and not at my father's? And Pau Tsu, be not ashamed."

The girl lifted radiant eyes.

"Listen," said she, "When you, during your vacation went on that long journey to New York, to beguile the time I wrote a play. My heroine is very sad, for the one she loves is far away and she is much tormented by enemies. They would make her ashamed of her love. But this is what she replies to one cruel taunt.

When Memory sees his face and hears his voice
The Bird of Love within my heart sings sweetly
So sweetly, and so clear and jubilant,
That my little Home Bird, Sorrow,
Hides its head under its wing,
And appeareth as if dead.

Shame! Ah, speak not that word to one who loves,
For loving, all my noblest, tenderest feelings are awakened,
And I become too great to be ashamed.

"You do love me then, eh Pau Tsu?" queried the young man.

"If it is not love, what is it?" softly answered the girl.

Happily chatting they descended the green hill. Their holiday was over. A little later Liu Venti was on the ferry boat which leaves every half hour for the western shore, bound for the Berkeley Hills, opposite the Golden Gate, and Pau Tsu was in her room at the San Francisco Seminary, where her father's ambition to make her the equal in learning of the son of Liu Jusong, had pleased her.

II

"I was a little fellow of just about their age when my mother first taught me to kow-tow to my father and run to greet him when he came into the house," said Liu Venti, speaking of the twins who were playing on the lawn.

"Dear husband!" replied Pau Tsu, "you are thinking of home — even as I. This morning I thought I heard my mother's voice, calling to me as I have so often heard her on sunny mornings in the Province of the Happy River. She would flutter her fan at me in a way which was all her own. And my father. Oh, my kind old father!"

"Aye," responded Liu Venti, "our parents loved us!"

"Let us go home," said Pau Tsu after a while.

Liu Venti started. Pau Tsu's words echoed the wish of his own heart. But he was not as bold as she.

"How can we?" he asked. "Have not our parents sworn that they will never forgive us?"

"The light within me today," replied Pau Tsu, "reveals that our parents sorrow because they have thus sworn. Liu Venti, ought we not to make our parents happy, even if we have to do so against their will?"

"I would that we could," replied Liu Venti, "but there is to be overcome your father's hatred for my father and my father's hatred for yours."

A shadow crossed Pau Tsu's face; but only for a moment. It lifted as she softly said: "Love is stronger than hate."

Little Waking Eyes ran up and clambered upon his father's knee.

"Me too," cried Little Sleeping Eyes, following him. With chubby fists he pushed his brother aside and mounted his father also.

Pau Tsu looked across at her husband and sons.

"The homes of our parents," said she, "are empty of the voices of little ones."

Three moons later, Liu Venti and Pau Tsu, with mingled sorrow and hope in their hearts, bade good bye to their little sons and sent them across the sea, offerings of love to parents of whom both son and daughter remembered nothing but love and kindness, yet from whom that son and daughter were estranged by a poisonous thing called Hate.

III

Two little boys were playing together on a beach. One gazed across the sea with wondering eyes. A thought had come — a memory. "Where is father and mother?" he asked, turning to his brother. The other little boy gazed bewildered back at him and echoed: "Where is father and mother?"

Then the two little fellows sat down in the sand and began to talk to one another in a queer little old fashioned way of their own. Their little mouths drooped pathetically; they propped their chubby little faces in their hands and heaved queer little sighs.

There was father and mother one time — always, always; father and mother and Sung Sung. Then there was the big ship and Sung Sung only, and the big water. After the big water, grandfathers and grandmothers, and Little Waking Eyes had gone to live with one grandfather and grandmother and Little Sleeping Eyes had gone to live with another grandfather and grandmother. And Little Waking Eyes and Little Sleeping Eyes had been good and had not cried at all. Had not father and mother said that grandfathers and grandmothers were just the same as fathers and mothers?

"Just the same as fathers and mothers," repeated Little Waking Eyes to Little Sleeping Eyes, and Little Sleeping Eyes nodded his head and solemnly repeated: "Just the same as fathers and mothers."

Then all of a sudden Little Waking Eyes stood up, rubbed his fists into his eyes and shouted: "I want my father and mother, I want my father and mother!" And Little Sleeping Eyes stood up and cried out strong and bold: "Let us go seek them. Let us go seek."

IV

So it happened that when the two new Sung Sungs who had been having their fortunes told by an itinerant fortune teller some distance down the beach, returned to where they had left their young charges, they found them not, and much perturbed, rent the air with their cries. Where could the children have gone? The beach was a lonely one, several miles from the seaport city where lived the grandparents of the children. Behind the beach, the bare land rose for a little way back up the sides and across hills to meet a forest dark and dense.

Said one Sung Sung to another, looking towards this forest: "One might as well search for a pin at the bottom of the ocean as search for the children there. Besides, it is haunted with evil spirits."

"A-ya, A-ya, A-ya!" cried the other, "Oh, what will my master and mistress say if I return home without Little Sleeping Eyes who is the golden plum of their hearts."

"And what will my master and mistress do to me if I enter their presence without Little Waking Eyes. I verily believe that the sun shines for them only when he is around."

For over an hour the two distracted servants walked up and down the beach, calling the names of their little charges; but there was no response.

V

Under the quiet stars they met — the two old men who had quarrelled in student days, and who ever since had cultivated hate for each other. The cause of their quarrel had long since been forgotten; but in the fertile soil of minds irrigated with the belief that the superior man hates long and well, the seed of hate had germinated and flourished. Was it not because of that hate that their children were exiles from the homes of their fathers — those children who had met in a foreign land, and in spite of their fathers' hatred, had linked themselves in love.

They spread their fans before their faces, each pretending not to see the other, while their servants enquired, "What news of the honorable little ones?"

"No news," came the answer from either side.

The old men pondered sadly and silently. Finally Liu Jusong said to his servants: "I will search in the forest."

"So also will I," announced Li Wang.

Liu Jusong lowered his fan. For the first time in many years, he allowed his eyes to rest on the countenance of his old college friend, and that one time friend returned his glance. But the servant men shuddered:

"It is the haunted forest," they cried. "Oh, honorable masters, venture not amongst evil spirits!"

But old Li Wang laughed them to scorn as also did Liu Jusong.

"Give me a lantern," bade Li Wang, "I will search alone. Thy grandson is my grandson and mine is thine."

"Aye," responded Li Wang.

And love being stronger than hate, the two old men entered the forest together, searched for their children together and found them together.

VI

"How many moons, Liu Venti, since our little ones went from us?" sighed Pau Tsu.

She was pale and sad and in her eyes was a yearning expression that had not been always there.

"Nearly five," returned Liu Venti.

"Sometimes," said Pau Tsu, "I feel I cannot any longer bear their absence."

She took from her bosom two little shoes, one red, one blue.

"Their first," said she. "Oh, my sons, my little sons!"

"Now, dear wife," said Liu Venti, "you must not grieve like that. The little ones are happy and all will some day be well."

A messenger boy approached, handed Liu Venti a message and slipped away.

Liu Venti read:

"May the bamboo ever wave. Son and daughter, return to your parents and your children."

Liu Jusong,

Li Wang.

A LOVE STORY FROM THE RICE FIELDS OF CHINA

CHOW MING, the husband of Ah Sue was an Americanized Chinese, so when Christmas day came, he gave a big dinner, to which he invited both his American and Chinese friends, and also one friend who was both Chinese and American.

The large room in which he gave the dinner presented quite a striking appearance on the festive evening, being decorated with Chinese flags and banners, algebraic scrolls, incense burners and tropical plants; and the company sat down to a real feast. Chow Ming's cook had a reputation.

Ah Ming and Ah Oi, Chow Ming's little son and daughter, flitted around like young humming birds in their bright garments. Their arms and necks were hung with charms and amulets given to them by their father's friends and they kept up an incessant twittering between themselves. They were not allowed, however, to sit down with their elders and ate in an ante room of rice and broiled preserved chicken — a sweet dish, the morsels of chicken being prepared so as to resemble raisins.

Chinese do not indulge in conversation during meal time; but when dinner was over and a couple of Chinese violinists had made their debut, the host brought forward several of his compatriots whom he introduced as men whose imaginations and experiences enabled them to relate the achievements of heroes, the despair of lovers, the blessings which fall to the lot of the filial and the terrible fate of the undutiful. Themes were varied; but those which were most appreciated were stories which treated of magic and enchantment.

"Come away," said Ah Sue to me. — We two were the only women present. — "I want to tell you a story, a real true love story — Chinese."

"Really," I exclaimed delightedly.

"Really," echoed Ah Sue, "the love story of me."

When we were snugly ensconced in her own little room, Ah Sue began:

"My father," said she, "was a big rice farmer. He owned many, many rice fields, but he had no son — just me."

"Chow Han worked for my father. The first time I saw Chow Han was at the Harvest Moon festival. I wore a veil of strings of pearls over my forehead. But his eyes saw beneath the pearls and I was very much ashamed."

"Why were you ashamed? You must have looked very charming."

Ah Sue smiled. She was a pretty little woman.

"I was not ashamed of my veil," said she, "I was ashamed because I perceived that Chow Han knew that I glanced his way.

"The next day I and my mother sat on the hill under big parasols and watched the men, sickle in hand, wading through the rice fields, cutting down the grain. It is a pretty sight, the reaping of the rice.

"Chow Han drove the laden buffaloes. He was bigger and stronger than any of the other lads. My mother did not stay by me all the time. There were the maid's tasks to be set. Chow Han drove past when my mother was not beside me and threw at my feet a pretty shell. 'A pearl for a pearl,' he cried, and laughed saucily. I did not look at him, but when he had passed out of sight I slipped the shell up my sleeve.

"It was a long time before I again saw the lad. My mother fell sick and I accompanied her to the City of Canton to see an American doctor in an American hospital. We remained in Canton, in the house of my brother-in-law for many months. I saw much that was new to my eyes and the sister of the American doctor taught me to speak English — and some other things.

"By the spring of the year my mother was much improved in health, and we returned home to celebrate the Spring Festival. The Chinese people are very merry at the time of the springing of the rice. The fields are covered with green, and the rice flower peeps out at the side of the little green blade, so small, so white and so sweet. One afternoon I was following alone a stream in the woods behind my father's house, when I saw Chow Han coming toward me."

Ah Sue paused. For all her years in America she was a Chinese woman.

"And he welcomed you home," I suggested.

Ah Sue nodded her head.

"And like a Chinese girl you ran away from the wicked man."

Ah Sue's eyes glistened mischievously.

"You forget, Sui Sin Far," said she, "that I had been living in Canton and had much talk with an American woman. No, when Chow Han told me that he had much respectful love in his heart for me, I laughed a little laugh, I was so glad — too glad for words. Had not his face been ever before me since the day he tossed me the shell?

"But my father was rich and Chow Han was poor.

"When the little white flowers had once more withdrawn into the green blades and were transforming themselves into little white grains of rice, there came to the rice country a cousin of Chow Han's who had been living for some years in America. He talked much with Chow Han, and one day Chow Han came to me and said:

"'I am bound for the land beyond the sea; but in a few years I will return with a fortune big enough to please your father. Wait for me!'

"I did not answer him; I could not.

"'Promise that you will ever remember me,' said Chow Han.

"'You need no primrose,' I returned. Chow Han set down the pot of fragrant leafed geranium which he had brought with him as a parting gift.

"'As for me,' said he, 'even if I should die, my spirit will fly to this plant and keep ever beside you.'

"So Chow Han went away to the land beyond the sea."

Ah Sue's eyes wandered to the distant water, which like a sheet of silver, reflected every light and color of the sky.

"Moons rose and waned. I know not how, but through some misfortune, my father lost his money and his rice farms passed into other hands. I loved my poor old father and would have done much to ease his mind; but there was one thing I would not do, and that was marry the man to whom he had betrothed me. Had not the American woman told me that even if one cannot marry the man one loves, it is happier to be true to him than to wed another, and had not the American woman, because she followed her conscience, eyes full of sunshine?

"My father died and my mother and I went to live with my brother-in-law in the city of Canton. Two days before we left our old home, we learned that Chow Han had passed away in a railway accident in the United States of America.

"My mother's sister and brother-in-law urged my mother to marry me to some good man, but believing that Chow Han's spirit was ever now beside me, I determined to remain single as the American woman. Was she not brighter and happier than many of my married relations?

"Meanwhile the geranium flower throve in loveliness and fragrance, and in my saddest moments I turned to it for peace and comfort.

"One evening, my poor old mother fell asleep and never woke again. I was so sad. My mother's sister did not love me, and my brother-in-law told me he could no longer support me and that I must marry. There were three good men to be had and I must make up my mind which it should be.

"What would I do? What should I do? I bent over my geranium flower and whispered: 'Tell me, O dear spirit, shall I seek the river?' And I seemed to hear this message: 'No, no, be brave as the American woman!'

"Ah, the American woman! She showed me a way to live. With her assistance I started a small florist shop. My mother had always loved flowers, and behind our house had kept a plot of ground, cram full of color, which I had tended for her ever since I was a child. So the care of flowers was no new task for me, and I made a good living, and if I were sad at times, yet, for the most part, my heart was serene.

"Many who came to me wished to buy the geranium plant, which was now very large and beautiful; but to none would I sell. What! barter the spirit of Chow Han!

"On New Year's day a stranger came into my shop. His hat partly concealed his face; but I could see that he was of our country, though he wore the dress of the foreigner and no queue.

"'What is the price of the large geranium at your door?' he enquired, and he told me that its fragrance had stolen to him as he passed by.

"'There is no price on that flower,' I replied, 'it is there to be seen, but not to be sold.'

"'Not to be sold! But if I give you a high price?'

"'Not for any price,' I answered.

"He sought to persuade me to tell him why, but all I would say was that he could not have the flower.

"At last he came close up to me and said:

"'There is another flower that I desire, and you will not say me nay when I put forth my hand to take it.'

"I started back in alarm.

"'You will not sell the geranium flower,' he told me, 'because you believe that the spirit of Chow Han resides within it. But 'tis not so. The spirit of Chow Han resides within Chow Han. Behold him!'

"He lifted his hat. It was Chow Han."

Ah Sue looked up as her husband entered the room bearing on his shoulder their little Han.

"And you named your boy after your old sweetheart," I observed.

"Yes," replied Ah Sue, "my old sweetheart. But know this, Sin Far, the Chinese men change their name on the day they marry, and the Chow Han, who gave me the scented leafed geranium, and after many moons, found me through its fragrance, is also my husband, Chow Ming."

CHAN HEN YEN, CHINESE STUDENT

I.

HE was Han Yen of the family of Chan, from the town of Choo-Chow, in the Province of Kiangsoo. His father was a schoolmaster, so also had been his grandfather, and his great grandfather before him. He was chosen out of three sons to be the scholar of the family, and during his boyhood studied diligently and with ambition. From school to college he passed, and at the age of twenty, took successfully the examinations which entitled him to a western education at government expense.

One of a band of Chinese youths he came to America and entered an American University. The new life and the new environment interested and exhilarated him. His most earnest desire was to absorb every good element of western education, so that he might be able to return to the Motherland well equipped to render her good service. He fully believed that he and his compatriot students were the destined future leaders of China, and his ambition to add lustre to the name of Chan, was almost holy.

The American widow with whom he boarded described him to her friends and neighbors as the best of all Chinese students. "And you know," she added with almost family pride, "the Chinese have the reputation of being the best students of all."

The widow, whose name was Mrs. Caroline Bray, had a daughter named Carrie. Carrie was a pretty girl of nineteen, with eyes and hair almost as dark as the eyes and hair of the little girl who had been adopted by Han Yen's parents to become his future wife. For seven months Carrie paid little attention to Han Yen. Her time was well occupied with housework, and in the evenings and Sundays, there was the Chinese Mission. Besides there were other students in the house.

It was one evening in early spring. The other Chinese students were dining a member of the Legation at a Chinese restaurant in the city, and Han Yen, who was unacquainted with the official, was alone with Mrs. Bray and her daughter. Mrs. Bray had been talking cheerily during the meal and Carrie had occasionally joined in. When Han Yen finally arose and was about to ascend the stairs to his room, the girl looked up with a smile and bade him not study too hard.

"What should I do with myself if I did not study?" asked Han Yen.

"Well," suggested Carrie brightly, "you might, for instance, come with me to the Chinese Mission sociable."

Han Yen had never before taken a walk with a young woman, but he had heard a paper read by a senior student, in which it had been stated that chatting with members of the fair sex, even though folly was their theme, should be part of the Chinese student's American curriculum. So politely expressing his pleasure at being permitted to accompany Miss Carrie, the boy put on his hat and solemnly walked down the street beside her.

Suddenly she began to laugh.

"What is amusing you?" he enquired.

"You walk too far away," she replied, "one would think you were afraid of me."

Han Yen, blushing and embarrassed, but desirous above all things of conforming to what was right and proper according to western ideas, lessened the distance between him and his companion.

The evening passed pleasantly if somewhat bewilderingly. On the way home the student learned from the youthful and self constituted missionary that through her instrumentality over one hundred Chinese boys had become acquainted with the English language and converted to Christianity.

"In behalf of my countrymen in America, accept my heartfelt gratitude," replied Han Yen.

The next afternoon, he repeated to his cousin, Chan Han Fong, what Miss Carrie had told him, adding: "I feel ashamed that a young female should be able to do so much more than I for the cause of humanity."

Though to Han Yen, Confucianist, the Missions certainly did not appeal as Temples of Ethical Culture, he was well able to appreciate the fact that they were the only bright spots in the lives of his laboring compatriots, exiles from their own homes and families.

After that evening Han Yen was invited occasionally to sit in the parlor of the widow Bray, where he listened to Carrie talking, playing, singing and otherwise entertaining her Chinese company. She was neither a clever nor well educated girl; but she was bright and attractive, and such as she was, dazzled the young student, to whom everything western, including women, was wonderful and worshipful.

One evening Carrie and Han Yen were alone. The girl was playing some sentimental melodies. The boy felt very happy. He always did feel happy when he was alone with Carrie. it was different when the other students were present, and Carrie smiled, first at this one, and then at that. Han Yen had not analyzed the painful sensations which took possession of him whenever Carrie smiled or spoke in friendly or familiar fashion to another student. On one occasion, however, these feelings had so overpowered him that he had risen abruptly from his seat and left the room. "Where are you going, Mr. Chan?" Carrie had called after him, and with innocent rudeness, he had replied: "To where you are not."

Carrie had returned to the room, demure and smiling. She understood Chinese students much better than they understood her, learned though they were and simple though she was.

This evening, for instance, she was fairly conscious of Han Yen's state of mind, and as she was a good natured little thing, continued playing for him for some time. Finally, she arose from the piano stool, and going over to the table on which stood a jar of hothouse flowers, took therefrom a piece of heliotrope.

"It was awfully sweet of you, Mr. Chan," said she, sniffing at the spray, "to bring me such beautiful flowers, and heliotrope is my favorite."

"It is very fragrant," murmured Han Yen.

"I had my fortune told yesterday," said Carrie, standing before the old fashioned mirror and fastening the flower in her hair.

"Was it a good one?" enquired the boy. Ordinarily he had no faith and little interest in mystical lore.

"I don't know," replied the girl, "it was rather funny, though. I don't think, Mr. Chan, that I shall tell you."

"I wish you would," urged Han Yen earnestly.

"Well, then, it was this: that my future husband would be a foreigner, and that he would bring me to-day a bouquet of flowers in which there would be one that was neither pink, yellow, green, blue nor red."

II.

When Chan Han Fong learned that his cousin loved a woman of the white race, and was resolved to do as the American men do when they fall in love, his face became pallid.

"What!" he cried, "you will relinquish your sacred ambition to work for China, dishonor your ancestors, disregard your parents' wishes, and set at naught your betrothal to the daughter of Tien Wang — all for sake of a woman of alien blood?"

"Yes," declared Han Yen, his face shining, "love is more than all."

"You have gone mad," cried Chan Han Fong, "think of the sorrow and disgrace which you will bring upon all to whom you are bound by the ties of relationship, gratitude and affection. Is a feeling which obliterates and destroys every virtuous thought and sentiment, worth cherishing?"

"The feeling which possesses me," replied Han Yen, "is divine."

Chan Han Fong stepped to his desk and took therefrom a paper: "Listen," said he, "six months ago you wrote:

Oh, China, misguided country!
What would I not sacrifice,
To see thee uphold thyself,
Among the nations,
For bitterer than death, 'tis to know,
That thou that wert more glorious than all,
Now lieth as low as the lowest,
Whilst the feet of those whom thou didst despise,
Rest insolently upon thy limbs,
The Middle Kingdom wert thou called,
The country that Heaven loves,
Thou wert the birthplace of the arts, the sciences,
And all mankind blessing inventions,

Thy princes rested in benevolence,
Thy wise men were revered,
Thy people happy.
But now, the empire which is the oldest
under the heavens is falling,
And lesser nations stand ready to smite,
The nation that first smote itself,
Truly Mencius has said:
'The loss of the empire comes through
losing the hearts of the people.'
The hearts of the people being lost,
Who shall restore the Empire?"

Silence followed this declamation. Chan Han Yen's face fell, bowed upon his hands.

"Alas for China!" exclaimed Chan Han Fong, his own young eyes glowing with fateful fire. "When those who know how she can and must be saved — the very ones who could and should be her saviours — turn traitor to her."

The bowed head was lifted.

"Oh, Fong," plead Han Yen, "I can no more be as I have been. The aim and purpose of my existence has changed. And what is one student to China?"

"Why are you here?" sternly demanded Chan Han Fong. Then, because his young cousin was dear to him, he went over to where the boy leaned, and laying his arm around his shoulder, pleaded with him thus:

"See, my cousin! The flowers of the fields and of the woods and dales! Those of a kind come up together. The sister violet companions her brother. Only through some mistake in the seeding is it otherwise. And the hybrid flower, though beautiful, is the saddest flower of all."

Han Yen trembled.

At that moment a girl's voice floated through the window.

"Yen, Yen," it called, "I want you to go into town with me."

Han Yen shook off his cousin's detaining hand.

"Pardon me," said he, "but I must go."

"Ah!" soliloquized Chan Han Fong, gazing sadly after him. "A low caste American girl has disordered his mind."

The year before Han Yen had come to the University, Han Fong had been invited, with several other Chinese students, to spend an afternoon at the home of a wealthy and cultured maiden lady who lived on the other side of the river. This lady, who was white haired, soft voiced and comprehending, had entertained the Chinese youths in what to them, was a most delightful fashion. Han Fong had never forgotten that afternoon, nor one who had been a part of and in harmony with it — a young girl, almost a child in years, tall and slender, with thoughtful eyes and quiet ways. That young girl had not belittled the foreign students by flirting with and plying them with numerous personal questions; but Han Fong had taken note that she had listened with interest while their hostess charmed them to talk of their work and aspirations, and that the few remarks which she had made, were intelligent, and proved, that young though she was, she understood the purpose of their lives and sympathised with it.

Because of that young girl, seen and heard but once, Chan Han Fong, called Carrie Bray, "low caste."

III.

Carrie had returned home tired out with a day's watching by the bedside of a sick Chinese woman.

"Why are you so good to everybody but yourself?" enquired Han Yen, meeting the girl as she entered the house in the dusk of the evening and following her into the sitting room.

"I *am* good to myself," answered Carrie cheerfully. "I'm accustomed to helping the poor Chinese. Indeed, I don't know what I shall do with myself after I give them up for you, Yen."

"I shall not require you to give them up altogether," replied the boy tenderly, "It is a work for humanity which you are doing and I hope to be able to help you with it."

"Why, dearie, what are you talking about?" exclaimed Carrie.

"About — when we shall be happy."

"You mean — when we go to China."

"No — here. I cannot go back to China for many years — perhaps never."

"Why?"

"Carrie's voice sounded sharp.

"Because I must work for my living — and for yours," answered the boy, "and if I were to return to China I would have to work for the government until I had repaid what I owed for my education here."

"Oh! Then you are not rich!"

"Rich!" echoed Han yen. "My father had to sell his land to enable me to complete my studies. Otherwise I would not have been able to compete at the Pekin examinations."

"You always used to say that you were going back to China."

"Yes," said Han Yen. "It was my great ambition to return to China and work for her — and alone I could have done so. But now, I shall not be alone — and I have a higher and loftier ambition than to work for China — it is to work for humanity — with you."

"I do not understand you," gasped Carrie.

"But you will," said Han yen. "Listen. I have yet to tell you how much I love you, and how all my heart is weeping and laughing for you. I am giving up all for you, to be with you, to work for you. I am not returning to my native land, because all my thought is you — and everything else is as naught."

The girl shrank before the rising emotion in the boy's face and voice.

"Good night, Yen, dear," said she, her hand upon the door knob, "I am so tired that I can't sit up one moment longer. See you to-morrow."

And then she stole away to the kitchen and said to her mother:

"What do you think? Yen's people are poor and after we are married, he will have to stay in America and live and work here just like a common Chinaman."

"Lands sakes!" ejaculated Mrs. Bray. "Ain't that awful! And I've been telling all around that you was to marry a Chinese gentleman and was to go to China and live in great style!"

"And he isn't a Christian either," murmured Carrie.

IV.

"Dear Friend:

Mother and I have been talking over things, and we have both decided that it would not be right for me to marry a man who is not a Christian. I am very sorry. I am going into town for a few days.

Your affectionate friend,

Carrie Bray."

Chan Han Yen read the little note over many times. Finally he folded it, put it back into its envelope and slipped it under the rubber band which bound together a neat bundle of letters lying on his desk.

Then he went out into the night. He did not know where he was going. All he knew was that the girl who had altered his life and driven everything else out of it, had cast him aside, because, oh, *not* because of the reason she had given. Chan Han Yen, Chinese student, was wiser than Carrie Bray in that respect.

His rage and mortification, his distress was indescribable. As he walked along he clenched his hands so that his nails sunk into his soft palms and the blood trickled down. He was only twenty-one.

Thus till morning dawned. The birds had begun to twitter when a turn in the road revealed a little hamlet lying in the semi-darkness of a valley. It was a peaceful scene and brought before the boy's mind his own home so far away — the home that he had been willing to cut himself away from forever. It seemed to him that he could see his father and his mother, his brothers, and the sweet little adopted daughter of the family. Yes, all the dear people who had been so proud of him, and who, one and all, had made so many sacrifices that he, the scholar, the talented one, might travel far and bring back to the east the wisdom of the west. To him they had trusted and

42

were trusting, to reflect honor and glory upon them and their country.

And he! Chan Han Yen threw himself down upon the soft turf. All anger and passion were spent; but in their place what shame and abasement of spirit! The air was sweet with the scent of the earth; the leaves hung silently on the bushes near by. Chan Han Yen fell asleep.

When he awoke the sun was well up. He turned his face to its brightness.

"Good morning, benign friend," said he, "the Lesson of the Woman is over."

CPSIA information can be obtained
at www.ICGtesting.com
Printed in the USA
LVHW020519290721
693949LV00008B/1178